A WOODLAND MYSTERY

The Mysterious I.O.U.

A WOODLAND MYSTERY
By Irene Schultz

Wright Group
McGraw-Hill

To my daughter-in-law Jeannie Hofeld, who
brings so much happiness

The Mysterious I.O.U.
Copyright ©2000 Wright Group/McGraw-Hill
Text by Irene Schultz
Cover illustrations by Meg Aubrey
Cameo illustrations by Taylor Bruce
Interior illustrations by Cheryl Kirk Knoll and Adam Weiskind

Woodland Mysteries® is a registered trademark of
Wright Group/McGraw-Hill.

Wright Group/McGraw-Hill
19201 120th Avenue NE, Suite 100
Bothell, WA 98011
www.WrightGroup.com

Printed in the United States of America

10 9 8 7 6 5 4 3 2

ISBN: 0-322-01962-1
ISBN: 0-322-02375-0 (6-pack)

What family solves mysteries ... has adventures all over the world ... and loves oatmeal cookies?
It's the Woodlanders!

Sammy Westburg (10 years old)
His sister Kathy Westburg (13)
His brother Bill Westburg (14)
His best friend Dave Briggs (16)
His best grown-up friend Mrs. Tandy
And Mop, their little dog!

The children all lost their parents, but with Mrs. Tandy have made their own family.

Why are they called the Woodlanders? Because they live in a big house in the Bluff Lake woods. On Woodland Street!

Together they find fun, mystery, and adventure. What are they up to now?

Read on!

Meet the Woodlanders!

Sammy Westburg
Sammy is a ten-year-old wonder! He's big for his fifth-grade class, and big-mouthed, too. He has wild hair and makes awful spider faces. Even so, you can't help liking him.

Bill Westburg
Bill, fourteen, is friendly and strong, and only one inch taller than his brother Sammy. He loves Sammy, but pokes him to make him be quiet! He's in junior high.

Kathy Westburg
Kathy, thirteen, is small, shy, and smart. She wants to be a doctor someday! She loves to be with Dave, and her brothers kid her about it. She's in junior high, too.

Dave Briggs

Dave, sixteen, is tall and blond. He can't walk, so he uses a wheelchair and drives a special car. He likes coaching high-school sports, solving mysteries, and reading. And Kathy!

Mrs. Tandy

Sometimes the kids call her Mrs. T. She's Becky Tandy, their tall, thin, caring friend. She's always ready for a new adventure, and for making cookies!

Mop

Mop is the family's little tan dog. Sometimes they have to leave him behind with friends. But he'd much rather be running after Sammy.

Table of Contents

Table of Contents

Chapter 1:
New Dog in Town

Ten-year-old Sammy yelled, "Hey, Freddy!
    "You want to come home with me for
lunch today?"

Freddy stopped at the end of the school hall.

Sammy caught up and said, "The pet show doesn't start until two o'clock.

"That gives us two hours to get the pets ready.

"I've got to give Mop a bath ... and brush out the knots from around his ears.

"And I'm going to make his collar fancy.

"Besides, we'd love to make lunch for you.

"You always tell us how good our sandwiches are.

"So do you want to come home and help me?"

Freddy Powell and Sammy Westburg were best friends in fifth grade.

They were exactly as tall as each other.

But Sammy was shaped sort of like a log.

And Freddy was shaped more like a stick.

Now Freddy wore a huge smile on his face.

Sammy thought, "What's going on with Freddy?"

Freddy said, "I can't go home with you today, Sammy.

"I have to go to our place and get MY pet ready."

Sammy said, "YOU'VE got a pet now? Hey, that's great!

"What is it?

"When did you get it?"

Freddy said, "Last Sunday.

"And it's a dog ... a beautiful dog ... a perfect dog."

Sammy said, "Hey, today is Thursday.

"Why didn't you tell me about it before?"

Freddy said, "Because I didn't know if

3

I would be allowed to keep him.

"My mom didn't decide 'yes' until yesterday.

"She said I have to earn all the money to take care of him.

"So I have to get a job ... and right away, too.

"See, here's how I got him.

"Mom's brother, my Uncle Moe, came to town last weekend.

"He's in the navy. Most of the time, he's aboard ship.

"But he visits us every year ... and he takes me places.

"Well, this year he took me to the county museum.

"And right next to the museum is the county dog pound.

"He loves animals just as much as I do, so we went in to look.

"Then he said I should choose one!"

Sammy said, "I thought your mom didn't want a dog around.

"Didn't she say a dog would be too hard to take care of?

"She and your dad both work at two jobs."

Freddy said, "I told Uncle Moe that, but he said he'd make it OK.

"And once I saw those dogs, I almost forgot what my mom said.

"We looked at every single dog in the pound.

"Every dog I saw, I thought, 'THAT'S the one I want!'

"There were big dogs ... too big for our little place.

"There were dogs so little ... they looked like they'd get hurt if you touched them.

"There were skinny dogs.

"And fat ones.

"And smooth ones.

"And hairy ones.

"And quiet dogs.

"And barking dogs.

"There were pure-bred dogs.

"There were mixed-breed dogs."

Sammy said, "How did you ever make up your mind?"

Freddy said, "Well, we came to the very last cage. And there was this dog.

"He was just sitting in the back.

"He looked out at me.

"He wagged his tail and tipped his head to one side ... like he was asking to be friends.

"I called, 'Hello there, dog,' and he trotted toward me.

"He sat down right in front of the cage door.

"He reached out a paw ... like he wanted to touch me.

"And right away I knew he was the one for me.

"My uncle paid the fee.

"He asked what kind of dog my dog was.

"The woman said she thought he was part toy collie and part poodle.

"And maybe some bulldog.

"And a couple of other kinds of dogs, too.

"I haven't named him yet. Right now, I just call him 'Dog.'"

Sammy said, "But what about your mom, Freddy?

8

"Wasn't she mad?"

Freddy said, "I was lucky. Mom really trusts her brother.

"And he told her I was old enough to take care of a dog ... and to do it all by myself!

"So yesterday, Wednesday, she finally decided I could keep him.

"So ... I'll see you at the pet show, Sammy."

Sammy said, "I can hardly wait to see your dog, Freddy.

"And my whole family except Dave will get to see him, too.

"Mrs. Tandy is coming.

"And Kathy and Bill are going to be here.

"The seventh and eighth grade classes are getting out early today just to see our pet show."

Freddy said, "What do you think the

surprise program at the end of the show is going to be?"

Sammy said, "I don't have a clue!

"All I know is that I can hardly wait until two o'clock!"

Chapter 2:
The Pet Show

The only rule for entering the pet show was very simple.

Every pet had to be on a leash or in some kind of cage.

Every pet would win an award just for being in the show.

The award was a paper with a big gold seal ... and the words:

I Took Part in the
Fourth & Fifth Grade

PET SHOW

A special ribbon would be given to each pet, too.

A ribbon for the pet with the longest tail.

One for the littlest pet and one for the biggest.

One for the dog that looked the least like a dog.

Ribbons for pets with the curliest hair.

Ribbons for dogs that minded their owners best.

Ribbons for pets that minded their owners worst.

There were ribbons for the pets with the funniest faces.

For the most colorful pets.

For pets with the biggest ears.

There were ribbons for the quietest pets.

And for the pets that made the strangest noises.

The principal was going to give out his own special ribbon.

It would be for the pet that looked the most like HIM!

The librarian, the gym teacher, and the principal would be the judges.

It was nearly two o'clock.

The pet show was going to start in just a few minutes.

Most of the kids were lining up, and Sammy was worried.

Freddy wasn't there yet.

A special pet-show school bus arrived.

Sammy ran to meet it ... but Freddy wasn't on it!

There wasn't much time left.

At last, Sammy spotted Freddy walking up the path.

He was following his dog.

Freddy called, "Sorry I'm so late. My dog needed exercise.

"And besides, I asked about jobs all the way here.

"But here's my dog. Isn't he the most wonderful dog?"

Sammy thought, "Is that a DOG?"

But what he said was, "He's great, Freddy!"

Freddy's dog was about the size of a toy collie.

It had tight little brown curls almost all over.

Its head was shaped like a bulldog's head ... with a pushed-in bulldog nose.

A wide white ring circled its left eye.

Its body was mostly brown, with spots all over ... tan and orange and white and black.

Its neck was ringed with smooth white hair, like a collie's.

Its tail was the strangest of all. It looked like a heavy black curled feather ... almost like a monkey's tail.

The dog wore a bright red leather collar.

Freddy was leading his dog by a man's belt.

Freddy said, "Mom gave me an old red belt. I made my dog's collar out of that."

Mop stood up and sniffed at the new dog's nose.

Then he licked it.

Sammy said, "Look, Mop likes your dog already."

Then they saw everyone lining up.

Sammy said, "Hey, we'd better get into line, too."

The boys began looking around at the other pets.

Freddy said, "Look over there.

"Martin has a snake ... in that huge

plastic bottle.

"And Asha has her mouse in that little tin cage."

They saw another girl, with a bird in a bamboo cage.

Then Sammy said, "Hey, look at Kim's guinea pig.

"I didn't know you could lead a guinea pig on a leash ... well, on a ribbon.

17

"And look at Bert's cat!

"He says it's the biggest cat in Bluff Lake."

Freddy said, "It looks like the biggest in the world!"

Sammy said, "One day I was at Bert's house.

"We put his cat into a cardboard box and weighed it.

"It weighed twenty-eight pounds ... twenty-seven when we took off a pound for the box."

Freddy said, "That's bigger than my cousin Latisha's BABY. And her baby's almost a year old."

Sammy said, "I looked up cats in a book of world records. There's a cat in England that weighs nearly forty pounds."

Suddenly, the boys heard a lot of talking behind them.

Sammy led Mop out of line to see what

was happening.

A minute later, he came running back to Freddy.

His hair was standing up every which way, like a weed patch.

His eyes were as big and round as coat buttons.

He said, "FREDDY! You won't believe what someone's brought to the school pet show!

"I only saw it from the back.

"I never knew anyone owned one, outside the zoo."

Freddy said, "Owned one WHAT, Sammy? What'd you see?"

Sammy said, "It's big and black like a huge black plastic leaf bag ... and it's thick-skinned ... and its legs are only about as long as a cell phone.

"And it has short, black hairs on its tail.

"You're gonna FAINT when you hear this, Freddy!

"Someone brought a RHINOCEROS, a baby rhinoceros, to school."

Chapter 3:
Bath Time

A second later, the crowd suddenly stopped talking.

A man walked up to the front of the line.

He was holding a box. It rattled as he shook it.

Sammy said, "That sounds like a rhythm band."

A small girl, Sandy Silver, followed the man.

She held a leash.

On it was a HUGE ... BLACK ... THICK-SKINNED ... SLOW-WALKING ... ANIMAL.

It was about four times as big as SANDY.

With every step the animal took, it grunted. "Umph. Umph. Umph. Umph. Umph."

Sammy thought, "HERE COMES THE BABY RHINOCEROS!"

But ... its face didn't look quite right for a rhinoceros.

There was no horn sticking out from the top of its nose.

And as it walked, its hanging belly

almost touched the ground.

Sammy thought, "Hey, it looks sort of like a ... PIG?"

Before he could be sure, something grabbed him from behind.

He tried to jump away, but he just couldn't.

The thing held on, and dragged him back a little.

The next second, a laughing voice said, "Ha! Gotcha!"

It was his fourteen-year-old brother, Bill.

Bill was a little taller than Sammy ... but built the same, heavy and strong.

Sammy said, "You brat! You almost made me step on Mop!"

Bill said, "Is that all the thanks I get?"

Sammy growled, "Thanks for what?"

Bill said, "For saving you from being eaten alive.

"That's a Vietnamese pot-bellied pig walking past you.

"What if it bites?"

Sammy was ashamed that he'd thought it was a rhinoceros. He didn't tell Bill.

He said, "I knew it was a Vietnamese pot-bellied pig.

"But I bet SOME kids thought it was a baby rhino."

Freddy just smiled and kept his mouth shut.

The kids at the front of the line began following the pig.

The parade circled around to the back of the school.

Bill joined his sister Kathy and Mrs. Tandy. They sat down on the lawn to watch.

The judges were sitting on folding chairs.

The gym teacher stood up.

24

She held a microphone.

She said, "Please lead all your pets over here ... past the judges' table.

"We have the awards and ribbons ready for them.

"And then get comfortable on the lawn for the special show.

"The program is, 'How to Bathe a Pot-bellied Pig.'

"Sandy Silver and her dad will show you how.

"But first, let me introduce you to their pig, Peewee.

"Please be as quiet as you can.

"Peewee might be worried around so many kids and animals.

"And he's not too happy about baths, either."

The kids walked their pets past the judges' table.

Freddy said, "Those ribbons are great. I wonder what OUR dogs are going to get."

The ribbon for the littlest pet went to a cricket.

The ribbon for the longest tail went to the snake.

Freddy's dog won a ribbon for the curliest hair.

Then Mop caught sight of Bill on the lawn.

Suddenly, he jerked the leash out of Sammy's hand.

He raced toward Bill.

Sammy shouted, "Here, Mop! Come here, Moppy! MOP!"

But Mop kept running till he reached Bill.

So Mop got a ribbon for being the dog that minded the worst.

The principal's award ... for the animal that looked most like him ... went to a bulldog.

Peewee was given a ribbon for making the strangest noises.

At last, every pet had its award and ribbon. It was time for the special show.

The Silvers led Peewee to some buckets standing ready.

Sandy said, "We wash Peewee every two weeks ... with the same shampoo WE use."

They poured shampoo onto two wet wash cloths.

They rubbed shampoo all over Peewee, except on his face.

He kept shifting from side to side and squealing.

Bill said, "With all the foam, he looks like a white pig."

Then the Silvers poured buckets of water over him.

He turned black again.

Mr. Silver said, "Now for Peewee's face.

"He just HATES to have his face washed."

Sandy dipped a washcloth into clear water.

Peewee's forehead had two big folds across it. They were so deep, they looked like a big pair of lips between his ears.

Sandy cleaned out the creases. Peewee squealed louder.

Sandy explained, "He can hardly see. These folds on his forehead hang way over his eyes.

"But I clean out the dirt in the folds.

"And I clean out the sticky stuff around his eyes."

Then she used the washcloth to clean out his ears.

They had black stuff in them. It looked like tar.

Peewee squealed even louder. He sounded like a broken horn.

Bill said, "This sounds like Sammy's bath, when he was little."

Finally, the Silvers dried Peewee off.

And then it was question-and-answer time.

Almost everyone had a hand in the air.

Sandy happened to call on Freddy first.

Freddy asked a question that no one expected.

Chapter 4:
Peewee the Pig

Freddy's question was, "Do you ever need anyone to help take care of Peewee?

"Because, if you do, I could do the job.

"I know a lot about pigs."

Mr. Silver said, "Why, as a matter of fact, we do!

"It's lucky you happened to ask right now.

"We planned a trip for this Saturday ... just for the day.

"It turns out our regular pig-sitter has the flu.

"So let's talk after the pet show is over."

Sammy whispered, "Freddy, I didn't know you knew any pigs."

Freddy said, "We used to live on a farm.

"We just had regular pigs, not pot-bellied ones.

"But I need work! And I need it bad! And I like pigs."

Bill said, "I bet you'd be a great pig-sitter. After all, you get along great with little piggy Sammy!

"But how come you're so eager to get work?"

Freddy said, "Well, I've got a dog to take care of now.

"And there's more than that. I can't tell you about it, but I need money FAST!"

By then, Peewee was munching on the grass.

Kids were waving their hands to ask questions.

One asked, "Why was your dad shaking that box?"

Sandy answered, "Because it's full of popcorn.

"And Peewee knows he will get popcorn if he follows it."

She emptied out the popcorn on the lawn.

Peewee squealed.

He sniffed for the popcorn and munched it up, fast.

Then he went back to chewing grass and leaves.

Another youngster asked, "Will he follow just on a leash?"

Sandy said, "Yes. But without popcorn rattling in front, he walks a lot slower."

Someone asked how old Peewee was.

Mr. Silver said, "He's around eight. We aren't sure.

"We used to know the exact date he was born ... but not now."

A girl asked, "How come you don't know it anymore?"

Mr. Silver said, "Because one day I left his birth certificate out ... and he ate it."

Everyone laughed.

A boy asked, "How much does Peewee weigh?"

Mr. Silver said, "The last time the vet weighed him, he was over two hundred pounds."

Bill asked, "How old was he when you got him?"

Mr. Silver answered, "He had just been weaned.

"He was no longer drinking milk from his mother.

"He was eight weeks old, and as long as my shoe."

As if he had heard, Peewee sniffed at Mr. Silver's shoe.

Someone asked what meals Peewee ate ... and when.

Sandy said, "He drinks two quarts of fruit juice a day. He doesn't drink water.

"And he gets a cup of pig pellets morning and night.

"And a bowl of oatmeal in the middle of the morning, about as much as you'd eat.

"And a bowl of cooked vegetables in the afternoon."

Sammy said, "Those pig pellets don't sound so great.

"I'm glad I'm not a Vietnamese pot-bellied pig."

Bill poked Sammy's belly and then whispered, "Oh, my mistake. I thought you WERE one!"

Sammy reached over and poked Bill back.

The principal called out, "Keep it calm over there!"

Sammy moved his hand and pretended he was only petting Mop.

Mr. Silver went on. "We give Peewee a little bit of ice cream for dessert ... but only about a fourth of a scoop."

Someone asked, "Does he know any tricks?"

Mr. Silver said, "At first, I was going to teach him tricks.

"Pigs are very smart, you know, smarter than dogs.

"Maybe you can guess why I decided not to."

One kid said, "Because he was a slow learner?"

That wasn't it.

Another youngster said, "Because you

had too many other things to do?"

That wasn't it.

Then Bill said, "Well, here's how I'd think.

"We have a dog, Mop.

"All we taught him is to be house-broken.

"He comes when we call ... well, some of the time.

"But he invented some tricks of his own.

"He rolls over to show you he's cute.

"And he touches your leg to get you to pet him.

"He sits up when he wants a piece of what you're eating.

"He's interesting just the way he is.

"Maybe you wanted to see what Peewee was like on his own."

Mr. Silver said, "That's exactly it, young man.

"Peewee learned to be housebroken right away.

"He uses a litter box, like a cat's but WAY bigger.

"When he was smaller, he'd climb the steps to my bedroom.

"Then he'd push his nose under my mattress. He wanted to dump me out of bed, to play."

Sandy said, "Now he climbs up next to Dad on the couch.

"He leans his head on Dad's shoulder to watch TV."

Mr. Silver said, "His bed is in the dining room.

"It's a piece of thick carpet, a sheet, and blankets.

"He lies down on it when he's tired.

"Then he grunts and squeals for us to cover him.

"And he grunts to thank us when we do."

Freddy whispered to Sammy, "I hope I get to pig-sit."

Sammy said, "I'll come over and help. It'll be fun!"

Bill said, "I'll help you guys, too, if you want me to."

Sammy said, "Forget it!

"I don't need my brother checking up on me ALL the time!"

That's what SAMMY thought!

Chapter 5:
The Invitation

It was four o'clock that afternoon. Dave
Briggs, the fifth member of the Woodland
family, drove into the garage.

He pulled his wheelchair from the seat behind him.

He lifted himself out of his hand-controlled van.

He lowered himself into the wheelchair.

Just then, the others got home from the pet show.

Kathy ran up to Dave. Together they wheeled up the ramp to the door.

Kathy opened the door.

All five Woodlanders rushed into the house.

They hurried into the kitchen for a snack of blueberry muffins.

Dave said, "How did the pet show go, Sammy?

"I'm sorry the high-schoolers didn't get to go.

"What kinds of animals showed up?"

Sammy said, "A LOT of animals! We had a great day.

42

"There were snakes ... birds ... a cricket ... guinea pigs ... dogs ... cats.

"One kid brought a big bowl of goldfish.

"There was even a Vietnamese pot-bellied pig!

"And tomorrow is ANOTHER great day.

"It's Friday, the county-wide TEACHERS' MEETING!

"NO SCHOOL! FOR ANYONE!"

Bill said, "Hey, everyone, you'll never guess what I'm going to do at two tomorrow afternoon."

Kathy said, "What?"

Sammy said, "Wait, wait, Bill, don't tell us.

"Let me guess.

"You're getting MARRIED!

"I saw you talking with Gale Winn yesterday.

"And she's DARLING!"

Sammy walked behind Bill's chair.

He put both hands on top of Bill's head.

He said, "Bill Westburg, I pronounce you pest and wife."

Bill laughed and said, "You're wrong, Sammy.

"But here it is.

"My teacher's giving extra credit to anyone who does a special report.

"It can be about any pet.

"You just bring the report in on Monday.

"Then BINGO! You get fifty extra points in science!

"Well, I've got something ALL of us could do."

Sammy stuffed another huge bite of muffin into his mouth.

He wrinkled up his nose.

He shook his head.

He said, "Count me out. No schoolwork for me!

"I'm going to play at the beach all day with Mop."

Bill said, "Gee, that's too bad, Sammy.

"I made a date to take Mop to the vet at two.

"And Dr. Jerome said we all can visit his clinic.

"You're invited, too, Sammy. But I'll

just tell him that you didn't want ... "

Sammy said, "Wait a minute! The vet clinic?

"Forget what I said!

"I was just kidding."

Kathy spoke up and said, "Do you think Dr. Jerome will let us watch him work?"

Dave said, "How come he invited us in the first place?"

Bill said, "Thank Mrs. Tandy for that.

"He bought cookies from her at the library sale.

"And he remembered her.

"And this morning when I called, he asked how she was.

"He said, 'I'd love to show Mrs. Tandy around, too.'

"Then he added, 'And bring the rest of your family.'"

Sammy started jumping around the kitchen.

He sang out, "Mrs. Tandy has a new BOY friend!

"Chief Hemster's gonna be MAA-aad. Just wait and SEE-ee!"

Bill laughed and said, "No, he's not, Sammy.

"Dr. Jerome and the chief are old friends.

"The doctor invited Chief Hemster, too.

"He said there's a mystery at the store next door.

"You know, the Messy Mutts Beauty and Pet Supply Shop?

"Well, Mrs. Peters owns it.

"And she is Dr. Jerome's sister.

"The chief told Dr. Jerome that we solve mysteries."

Dave said, "Did he tell you what the problem is?"

Sammy asked, "Is a dog having a bad hair day?"

47

Bill laughed and said, "No, that's not it.

"Someone's been inside of Mrs. Peters's shop.

"She doesn't know who.

"The funny part is this: she wouldn't even have noticed.

"But she found a mysterious note."

Sammy screeched, "There's a MYSTERI-OUS NOTE?

"WHY DIDN'T YOU TELL US RIGHT AWAY, YOU BIG GOOF!"

He tipped Bill's chair sideways and dumped Bill onto his feet.

Bill said, "Why did you do that, you monkey?"

Sammy didn't answer.

He just grabbed Bill by the arm and pulled him down the hall.

He said, "Wait till you see what I've been saving up for this exact moment!"

Chapter 6:
The Great Detective
Is Ready

Sammy ran into his bedroom.

He grabbed a bunch of pencils from the top of his desk.

He opened a drawer.

He pawed through it like a dog digging for a bone.

Finally, he dug out five pocket-sized notebooks.

He handed a pencil and a notebook to Bill.

Then he dumped another drawer out onto the floor.

Out spilled a pile of plastic bags ... all different sizes.

He stuffed some into Bill's back pocket.

Bill said, "What are all these bags for?"

Sammy said, "They're our evidence bags.

"Don't you remember the detectives on TV?

"They're always pulling out evidence bags.

"And pocket notebooks.

"And pencils, to write where they find the evidence."

Sammy began pawing around in ANOTHER drawer.

He pulled out two little, round, flat, soft plastic cases.

Bill said, "Hey, those are the family magnifying glasses! I thought they were lost."

Sammy dug out another magnifying glass ... a little one that had a black handle.

And then he found another like it, but larger.

And a tube-shaped magnifier.

Bill said, "Why, you little pack rat!

"So THIS is where ALL the magnifying glasses went! YOU took them.

"They're supposed to be in the chest in the dining room ... by our stone collection!"

Sammy said, "I didn't TAKE them. I COLLECTED them.

"See, I'm reading a book about crime
labs.

"So I figured WE should have the
things they have ... to take to our next
mystery.

"Now, come on. Let's hand this stuff
out to the family.

"And let's do our weekend homework
tonight.

"And let's go to Dr. Jerome's early, BE-
FORE two o'clock.

"And then I will lead you to the Messy
Mutts Shop.

"There we will solve ... "

Here Sammy boomed out in a loud,
deep voice, "THE MYSTERY AT THE MESSY
MUTTS!"

Bill groaned, "I can see that tomorrow
... with the great detective Sammy leading us ... is going to be a long, long day."

■   ■   ■

Friday, before two, the family piled out of Dave's van. He had parked in front of the Messy Mutts Beauty and Pet Supply Shop.

Kathy climbed out, carrying little, sleepy Mop.

Mrs. Tandy said, "Look at Mop's nose. It's wiggling, but he's still asleep.

"I bet it's because he smells the other dogs."

Bill said, "Remember the last time Mop ran away?

"We searched all over Bluff Lake for him.

"He'd trotted all the way to Green Forest, to Dr. Jerome's.

"He just loves being with the other dogs."

Kathy carried Mop inside.

The doctor's helper took them right to a back room.

There stood the doctor, holding two needles in his hand.

Chief Hemster was with him.

Mrs. Tandy said, "Why hello, John. And hello again, Doctor.

"How nice of you to invite us over today."

Dr. Jerome said, "A great cookie-maker is always welcome."

Mrs. Tandy said, "Well, you're praising the wrong person.

"Sammy baked all those great cookies.

"I was just selling them for the library fund."

The doctor said, "Well then, Sammy can be my helper.

"Here, Sammy, you can hold Mop on this table."

Sammy said, "Hey, not me. I'm going to be the world's greatest detective.

"I hate needles.

54

"But Kathy would love to help. She's going to be a doctor."

Kathy walked over and held Mop. Dr. Jerome gave him the shots.

He patted Mop and said, "That's it, little fellow."

Carefully, he lifted Mop down to the floor.

Then he said, "Well, suppose you all go next door now.

"Talk to my sister and find out what's wrong over there.

"I'll take care of some of my patients.

"Then we can talk at the café across the street, around three.

"They have the best sweet rolls in town.

"I go there every single day to get one.

"And after that, you can come back here.

"I can show you around the hospital a little then."

Sammy said, "Dr. Jerome, if you get to go for sweet rolls every single day, well ... maybe giving shots isn't SO awful.

"I think I'm going to be a detective AND a vet."

Chief Hemster laughed and said, "Well, I have to get back to Bluff Lake now.

"But I'll meet you at the café."

So the family went next door ... to learn about the mystery at the Messy Mutts.

MESSY MUTTS
BEAUTY & PET
SUPPLY SHOP

Chapter 7:
The Strange Note

Kathy tied Mop outside the Messy Mutts'
big front window.

They wanted to be able to see him
easily.

Mrs. Peters was waiting for them inside.

The Woodlanders said hello and told her their names.

She said, "I'm so glad you've come. Chief Hemster told my brother all about you.

"I have a mystery that I can't begin to solve."

The family looked around.

The Messy Mutts Shop was one room ... it stretched from the front window to the back door.

Shelves of supplies lined the front walls.

Cages for waiting dogs lined the back walls.

Toward the back were four waist-high metal tables.

Mrs. Peters said, "Those are where dogs are clipped.

"Only the person doing the clipping is allowed back there."

Mrs. Peters talked and darted around the shop at the same time.

She un-wrapped and hung up new dog leashes.

She picked up a huge cardboard box from the counter.

She emptied it into a bin marked "Dog Cookies."

Mrs. Tandy said, "That's a heavy load ... and you're no bigger than a bird, Mrs. Peters."

Mrs. Peters said, "Call me Liz. Everyone does.

"My brother jokes that Liz is short for lizard ... because I'm little and I move so fast."

She pushed up one sleeve of her blue work shirt.

She made a muscle and said, "I HAVE to work fast.

"There's a lot to do ... and no one else

here to do it.

"I've been looking for someone to help after school."

Dave said, "Why don't you take a rest for a minute? Tell us what happened."

Liz said, "I guess I can use a break."

Sammy said, "Wait, wait a second. Don't start yet!

"You guys, take out your notebooks first."

Liz laughed. "The chief told me you solve mysteries.

"But he didn't tell me Sammy was boss.

"Now, let's see, what should I tell you first?

"I guess I'll start with Tuesday morning at ten.

"My next dog wasn't due in for a bath and clipping yet.

"I had half an hour free.

"I decided to catch up on the bills.

"I use the desk in the corner for sending out bills."

The Woodlanders followed her over to the desk.

She said, "Here's where I found it ... right on top of this pile of papers."

Sammy said, "Found what?"

Liz said, "This note."

They crowded around to see the paper she picked up.

She handed it to Dave. He read it out loud. Here is what it said:

Dave turned the paper over to the other side.

He said, "There's no name signed on either side.

"And it doesn't say how much will be paid back."

Liz said, "But the note isn't the only mystery.

"How long it's been on my desk is a mystery, too.

"You see, I only send out bills a few times a month.

"The last time I did it was two weeks ago.

"That I.O.U. could have been here for two days or two weeks ... and I just didn't see it.

"Besides, I can't understand how it got there.

"Or why any stranger would owe me money."

Bill asked, "Do you have ANY idea who left it?"

Liz said, "Not a hint."

Mrs. Tandy said, "Do you have anyone helping you here?

"Someone who might have seen how the note got in?

"Who might even have written it?"

Liz said, "I do have one helper, Jane. She works four mornings a week.

"She washes and clips dogs.

"I asked her about the note when she came in yesterday.

"She doesn't know anything about it."

Sammy said, "How could it get inside? Do you lock your doors every night?"

Liz said, "Oh my, yes.

"I have so many supplies ... I'd be put out of business if they were stolen.

"But it seems to me that they're all still here."

63

The Woodlanders looked around.

There were dog and cat collars ...
    leashes
    bags of pet food
    bags of cat litter
    pet toys
    all sizes of chew-bones
    bottles of shampoo
    metal and plastic collar tags
    big and little feeding bowls
    two aquariums of fish
... and hundreds of other things.

Dave said, "Well, let's take a look at the note again.

"Maybe there's something we can find out from it."

He stared at it for a minute.

Then suddenly he blurted out, "Hey! Look at what this thing is written on."

Chapter 8:
What's Wrong with Sammy?

Everyone crowded around Dave for a better look.

Dave said, "Look at this piece of paper! Isn't it from a school assignment book?"

Sammy said, "Yeah. You're right. One just like mine."

Kathy said, "Do you think a kid wrote this note?

"Because who else would have an assignment book?"

Liz said, "But I would have noticed a youngster in the back of my shop.

"And I haven't seen anyone."

Bill said, "That handwriting is really good.

"Some girls have neater writing than boys. Maybe a girl wrote that."

Sammy said, "I don't know about that.

"Some guys I know have GREAT hand-writing.

"You know my friend Freddy? He has the best in the class.

"It's as good as the writing on this note."

Dave said, "We aren't getting anywhere

with this.

"Let's stop asking who wrote the note.

"And when it was left here.

"And how it got here.

"Let's start with some other kinds of questions.

"Let's figure out WHY someone left an I.O.U.

"Could ANYthing be missing that you didn't notice, Liz?

"Or could you have left the shop un-locked one night ... with maybe some money lying around?

"Or did you notice ANYthing at all that was strange?"

Liz said, "No, I take my money to the bank every night.

"But ... there was one thing that was a little unusual. You'll probably laugh.

"Monday morning, I found a few pieces of dry dog food on the floor.

"Just a few, right near all those dog food bags."

Sammy said, "I'd think you'd find that around a lot."

Liz said, "Oh no. Those bags are almost airtight.

"And I clean the floor every night before I leave.

"I sweep it VERY carefully. And I wet-mop, too.

"I'm sure I did both before closing the night before.

"So dry dog food on the floor was a surprise."

Kathy asked, "Were any of the dog food bags torn?"

Liz said, "I checked, but they all were OK.

"I couldn't figure out how that food got there."

Then Dave said, "Let's see if there's a

clue on the back of this note."

He turned the paper over.

They all looked at what was written on the back.

Dave read it aloud.

SS 27, 2-4-6-8-10
E 89, 66-67

Sammy got very excited.

He said, "Oh boy! I bet that's a code!

"'SS' stands for Secret Service maybe! And I bet 'E' stands for some thing important.

"Maybe EMERGENCY!

"And look at the rest of the words, below the code."

Bill read them off.

Cookie
Jumping Bean
Muffin
Monkey

Mrs. Tandy said, "Maybe that's a shopping list?"

Dave said, "But where do you shop for a monkey? And how about a jumping bean?"

Just then, they heard the noise of a big motor.

It sounded as if it were right inside of the shop.

Mrs. Tandy said, "My goodness, what's that?"

Liz laughed. "Don't be scared.

"It's a delivery truck driving by in the back alley.

"I have a bird feeder out there. It has a microphone in it to pick up birds' sounds.

"I set the mike on low, so we could talk easily.

"But even on low, it picks up some noise."

Kathy said, "We have a bird feeder like that.

"It's a little house with a microphone inside.

"We mounted ours on a post in the backyard.

"We can hear the birds pecking and singing."

Liz said, "My feeder's mounted right above the back door.

"The birds don't seem to mind when someone drives by.

"I leave the microphone on all the time.

"I don't even turn it off when I leave.

"It's so nice to hear birds first thing in the morning.

"Well, I don't hear that truck out there anymore.

"I'll just turn the mike back up for the day."

She re-set a pointer on a small box on her desk.

Bill said, "I think it's time for sweet rolls."

They left the shop, and Liz locked up.

Kathy took Mop by the leash.

They all went on talking about the strange I.O.U. ... everyone except Sammy, that is.

Sammy ... usually the biggest talker of the family ... was strangely silent.

Bill wondered, "Is Sammy sick?"

Chapter 9:
Pets Can Get Mean

They crossed over to the café.

Chief Hemster and Dr. Jerome were waiting for them.

Dr. Jerome asked the waitress, "What kinds of sweet rolls do you have today?"

The waitress said, "All kinds, and we have jelly donuts."

The others chose, but Sammy said, "Any kind."

Bill poked him and said, "Hey! Didn't you hear?

"They have JELLY DONUTS! Your favorite!"

Sammy said, "Stop poking, you pest! I'm thinking!"

So the waitress brought him a plain sweet roll.

Dr. Jerome said, "Well, Woodlanders, what did you discover?

"I had to go help a sick cow when Liz called me.

"So all I know is that she found a mysterious note."

Bill said, "The truth is, we didn't find

much more."

Dave said, "And what we did find doesn't make sense."

Mrs. Tandy said, "But we made copies of the note.

"We can look them over carefully tonight."

Kathy said, "And we have our notebooks to go through."

Sammy said, "But we won't report until Sunday. See, I'll be away from home tomorrow.

"And the family can't figure out much without me."

Bill groaned at that, but Sammy ignored him.

He said, "I'm helping take care of a pig Saturday.

"And Peewee's owners won't get home until around six.

"I'll be off the case until dinnertime."

The doctor said, "Peewee? I know Peewee!

"I'm his vet!

"And I'm warning you now: don't make him mad!

"If you get Peewee mad, watch out! Pets can get mean."

Right then, a cell phone in the doctor's pocket rang.

He answered it and listened for a moment.

Then he said, "A dog's hurt himself on a wire fence.

"I'll have to sew him back up. Come on."

Dr. Jerome paid and hurried out of the café. Chief Hemster and the Woodlanders hurried after him.

Sammy hadn't eaten even one bite of his sweet roll.

Bill thought, "Now I KNOW Sammy is sick."

Everyone crossed the street to the animal hospital.

The doctor said, "Put Mop into one of those cages.

"He will be out of the way there, and safe."

Then the doctor and his nurse washed up.

They pulled on plastic gloves.

Kathy said, "It seems like operating on people.

"Except animals can't tell you where they hurt.

"And besides, they might try to bite their doctor!"

The doctor's helper brought in a small white poodle.

One of its shoulders was red with blood.

Dr. Jerome gave the dog some shots.

He said, "Those will stop pain and infection ... and calm him."

The doctor trimmed off some bloody fur.

Under the fur was a deep cut, about two inches long.

The doctor washed the cut.

The nurse handed him a threaded needle.

He sewed together the torn muscle

under the skin.

He said, "These stitches won't have to be taken out. This thread disappears all by itself."

He used different thread for the outside stitches.

Finally, he put a bandage on the dog's shoulder.

He fitted a wide plastic collar around its neck ... to keep it from biting at the stitches.

He said, "He should be fine.

"I don't think you'll find much else exciting here today.

"I'll examine the animals waiting to see me, and ... "

Suddenly, they heard loud voices in the waiting room.

A firefighter rushed in.

He was carrying a crying boy about six years old.

A man and a woman hurried in with them.

They were holding up the boy's right hand.

Something the size of a softball seemed stuck to one of the boy's fingers.

The firefighter said, "We need help, Doc, right away!

"Larry, here, kept poking his pet box turtle. In its soft part. Between its shells.

80

"After a while, the turtle had enough of that!

"It squeezed its shells together on Larry's finger.

"And it won't let go.

"His folks tried everything ...

pulling the shells apart

tapping on the turtle

shaking it

... offering it food."

By now, Larry was howling.

The dogs waiting in the cages began howling.

Dr. Jerome stopped to think for just a second.

Then he rushed across the room.

He wheeled a cart over to the howling boy.

The cart had a tank on top of it.

A thin rubbery hose stuck out of the tank's side.

The doctor held the end of the hose near the turtle's nose.

He turned a valve to "on" for just a moment.

He fanned his hand in the air near the turtle's head.

In a second, the turtle's bottom and top shells moved apart.

Larry pulled out his finger.

But the turtle lay still, its eyes closed.

Sammy said, "Oh, no, Doc! You've killed it!"

Chapter 10:
Get That Sample!

The doctor laughed. "Don't be silly, Sammy.

"I haven't killed it.

"I gave it a little puff of laughing gas.

"That made it relax so it had to let go.

"The turtle's OK.

"But Larry's finger will be sore for a while."

Sure enough, there was a blood blister on it.

At first, Larry's mother hugged and kissed him.

She said, "I was afraid you'd never get loose."

He held up his finger for her to look at.

He expected she would feel sorry for him.

But instead, she got MAD!

She said, "Of COURSE the turtle would close up like a box!

"Why else would he be called a 'box turtle'?"

And Larry's father said crossly, "How would you like someone poking at YOU?

"You should NEVER poke a poor little animal."

Sammy whispered to Bill, "You SEE, Bill? Keep poking me, and guess what'll happen to YOU!"

Finally, Larry and his folks left.

Doctor Jerome said, "Too bad, but now there isn't time to show you around.

"I hope you all come back on some other day."

The Woodlanders and Chief Hemster thanked the doctor and left.

The minute they were outside, Sammy said, "I'm hungry.

"It's all your fault, Bill.

"You let me order the wrong kind of sweet roll.

"You KNOW I like jelly donuts best of all!"

"So here's the poke I owe you ... for the last poke you gave me."

Bill said, "Hey, don't blame me!"

Chief Hemster said, "Sammy, why are you so cross?

"Don't you remember that Bill wanted you to get a jelly donut? But you wouldn't.

"So something else must be bothering you."

Sammy began to feel a little ashamed.

He said, "I guess I'm angry ... and hungry from worrying my brains out."

He pulled a piece of paper out of his pocket.

"You know the handwriting on this I.O.U.?

"I've been looking at it ... and now I'm SURE it's Freddy's.

"And he's my best friend in fifth grade.

"And it looks like he's up to something crooked.

86

"But I don't want to hurt his feelings by accusing him. Because may be he didn't do anything wrong."

Chief Hemster said, "Listen here, Sammy. You could still be IMAGINING it's his.

"After all, you don't have a sample to compare it to.

"So why don't you drop the subject for today.

"Let's all go out for an early dinner together."

Bill said, "Yeah. Maybe things will look different to you after you've had a hamburger.

"Then tomorrow you'll be busy with Freddy.

"Maybe you can get a handwriting sample ... without hurting his feelings."

■　■　■

The Woodlanders were home by six o'clock.

Kathy said, "Do you feel any better now, Sammy?"

He said, "A little. Let's all go over the notes we made this afternoon.

"Maybe we can figure out what to do next."

By bedtime, they had written this list:

Some one—
  got into Liz's shop.
  probably got in at night.
  didn't use the doors ... so there MUST be
an other entrance.
  (Find that entrance.)
  wrote an I.O.U. ... so someone took SOME thing.
  used an assignment book ... so we think a kid
wrote the note.
  The kid spilled dry dog food.
  None of the bags was broken into (so was there
AN OTHER bag?)
  Did the kid TAKE a bag? ... Check with Liz to
see if one is missing.
   The kid wrote a message in code.

Dave sat looking at the last entry.

Suddenly he said, "Hey, wait a minute! I know what that CODE is all about!

"And it isn't about the Secret Service at all.

"I bet you have 'SS' in your assignment book, Sammy. And numbers, too."

Sammy ran to get his assignment book.

He opened it and said, "Wow! You're right.

" 'SS' is for social studies.

"And the numbers mean to do page 27, questions 2, 4, 6, 8, and 10.

"And 'E' 89, 66–67 is my English assignment.

"And that makes everything worse!

"Because now I know this for sure: whoever wrote that I.O.U. note is in my class.

"And that means it probably COULD have been Freddy.

"What will I say to him when I see him tomorrow?"

Bill said, "Well, whatever you say ... be sure to get that sample of his writing!

"And if it turns out he IS in trouble ... well, then maybe we can help him."

Chapter 11:
Trouble with Peewee

By the next morning, Sammy's mind was
made up.

HE WOULD FIND A WAY TO GET THAT
WRITING SAMPLE!

He met Freddy at the Silvers' house.

Freddy said, "Am I glad you're here, Sammy!

"I brought my dog. Just look out that window.

"He's tied to a tree. I finally named him ... Monkey!"

Sammy thought, "Monkey? Where did I just see that word?"

Freddy said, "It's time for Peewee's breakfast.

"He eats this bowl of pig chow outside the door. Then he walks around.

"He thinks he owns this place, so he stays on the lot.

"He checks things out and eats a little grass.

"Then he scratches on the door to come in."

In a flash, Sammy came up with Handwriting Plan Number One.

He said, "Why don't we play Hangman while we wait for him?

"You can have the first turn, so you write first."

But Freddy said, "I can't right now, Sammy.

"I have to check on Monkey's water, and his rope.

"And I have to lay out clean blankets for Peewee's bed."

Sammy breathed a sigh of relief. He felt guilty about trying to trick his friend.

In a few minutes, they heard a loud scratching.

They let Peewee into the house. He lay down on his bed in the dining room.

He squealed happily as the boys covered him.

Sammy thought, "Well, time to try Handwriting Plan Number Two. But I hate to do it."

93

He said, "Why don't you write a list, Freddy ... so I know what we have to do today?"

Freddy said, "Oh, there's a list already, from Mr. Silver.

"There on the counter, by that pencil."

So the great detective's second plan was no good. Secretly, he felt glad.

Then Freddy said, "Let's play games in the family room."

Sammy thought, "There's a third plan! I'll just find us a writing game!"

But there WERE no writing games around.

Sammy breathed another sigh of relief. He thought, "We really need that sample ... but I feel TERRIBLE, trying to sneak one over on Freddy."

Then Freddy said, "It's time to feed Peewee again."

Sammy frowned as he followed Freddy

back into the kitchen.

Freddy took out a package of dry oatmeal.

He laid it on a chair. He looked for a microwave bowl.

In walked Peewee ... and THAT'S when things began to go wrong.

Peewee saw the package. He grabbed it in his teeth.

He carried it out into the family room.

He stepped on it with one hoof. He ripped it open.

Out spilled a mess of tan oatmeal onto the green rug.

Sammy said, "Freddy! Come quick! We'd better vacuum that up!

"Look, he's eating it. What if he eats the rug, too ... like he eats grass?"

Sammy and Freddy ran and found a vacuum cleaner.

They plugged it in. They turned it on.

The next instant, they heard a terrible snorting.

Peewee came charging right at them!

His lips were pulled back.

His big sharp teeth were showing.

He looked MAD!

Sammy pulled out the plug. He grabbed Freddy's arm and they ran to the kitchen.

Peewee dashed after them. The boys jumped onto a chair.

Peewee ran at the chair, biting at it.

The boys climbed up on top of the counter.

They pulled their legs up tight and hugged their knees.

Peewee leaned his front legs against the cabinets ... and snapped at their feet.

Sammy said, "I'm not getting down while he's in this ROOM!"

Twenty minutes later, Peewee was still snapping.

Freddy said, "What about feeding Peewee?

"And what if he has to go?"

Sammy said, "What about feeding US guys?

"And what if WE have to go?"

Then he saw how worried Freddy was.

He said, "It'll be OK, Freddy. I'll think of something."

And that's when Freddy saved Sammy from having to think of another plan.

Freddy said, "Hey, Sammy, we might as well be doing something.

"We could be writing that poem for English next week.

"We signed up to do it together. Let's start on it now."

He slid over and got the pad and pencil from off the counter.

He slid back and said, "Let me do the writing."

"Now, the poem's supposed to be about something you play with. I was thinking of writing about a balloon."

Sammy said, "I like that! A balloon is a wonderful thing!"

Freddy said, "Hey, that could be our first line."

After half an hour, they had their poem:

A balloon is a wonderful thing.
All over it's round as a ring.
It follows its friends
to their tragical ends,
and then all that's left
is its string.

Freddy said, "I'm not sure 'tragical' is a word."

Sammy said, "It is now."

Freddy said, "Here, Sammy. You'll want to take this ... to make yourself a copy."

Sammy folded the paper and put it into his pocket.

Then Freddy said, "I want DOWN, Sammy! Peewee, get OUT of here!"

Then, like magic, the doorbell rang ... and Peewee walked to the front hall to see who was there.

Sammy and Freddy sneaked down from the counter.

Their legs felt all pins and needles ... but they moved fast.

Quietly they closed all the doors to the front hall.

Now Peewee was TRAPPED! And the boys were FREE!

They ran to the back door. Sammy hollered out, "Who's there?"

Bill walked into the yard. He said,

"Don't get mad, Sammy.

"I just rode over to make sure you guys were doing OK."

Mad? Sammy grabbed Bill and hugged him like an octopus.

Then the two boys told Bill what had happened.

Bill rode right home and made popcorn.

He brought back two big paper bags of it, and a box.

Now they knew they'd get Peewee to mind them.

And Sammy had Freddy's handwriting sample at last.

Was it the same as on the I.O.U. note?

Chapter 12:
In the Dark

The Silvers finally came home.

They were SO sorry about how Peewee had acted.

They knew that he hated the vacuum cleaner ... but they never thought the boys might turn it on.

They paid Freddy. They gave him extra pay for the trouble Peewee had caused.

Sammy and Freddy went out. It was just turning dark.

They un-tied Monkey and started walking.

With one hand, Freddy held on to Monkey's rope.

His other hand rested in his pocket. He held his pig-sitting money in his fist.

Sammy walked with a hand in each pocket.

He held the I.O.U. in one hand. In the other, he held Freddy's handwriting sample.

The writing on both was the same. Sammy felt awful.

Freddy said, "Sammy, you helped me

so much today. But I need another favor.

"I have to pay back some money ... in a dark place.

"Could you walk there with me, and wait outside?

"It's in Green Forest, right near where I live.

"You could use my flashlight to go home."

Sammy said, "Freddy, I have to tell you something.

"Somebody broke into the Messy Mutts Shop.

"They left a note.

"Mrs. Peters asked my family to find out who left it.

"I think the handwriting on the note is yours.

"And the name Monkey is on the back of the note.

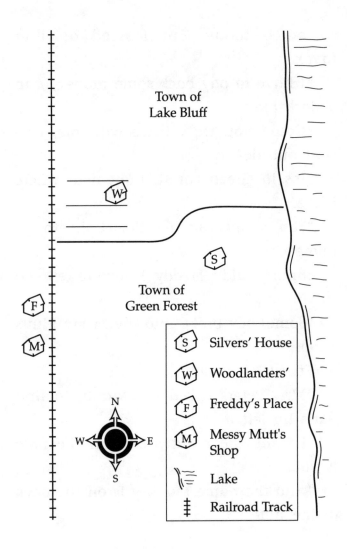

Town of
Lake Bluff

Town of
Green Forest

ⓢ	Silvers' House
ⓦ	Woodlanders'
ⓕ	Freddy's Place
ⓜ	Messy Mutt's Shop
〰	Lake
‡	Railroad Track

"So I have to ask you ... are you a crook?"

Freddy said, "Aw, come on, Sammy. I'm not a crook.

"I'm not even the one who did the break-in ... or not at first.

"But I AM the one who left the I.O.U.

"Just go to the shop with me for a minute, will you?

"Then I promise I'll explain how everything happened."

Sammy thought that over.

Then he said, "OK, if my family can meet us there."

Freddy thought that over.

Then he said, "OK. If you'll help me keep this quiet.

"If my folks hear, they might not let me keep Monkey."

So Sammy called his family from a pay phone.

Then he and Freddy walked on toward the Messy Mutts.

In a few minutes, they were a block away.

Now it was VERY dark.

Freddy pushed Monkey's rope into Sammy's hand.

He said, "Here, Sammy. Hold on to Monkey for me."

Then he darted off.

Sammy ran after him, pulling Monkey along.

He called, "Wait, Freddy. Listen to me!

"You don't HAVE to sneak inside in the dark.

"You can give the money to Mrs. Peters tomorrow.

"She's nice. I bet she won't be mad at you."

But Freddy had disappeared in the darkness.

Just then, the Woodlanders drove up. Bill jumped out.

He said, "Sammy, do we have news for YOU!

"We drove here this afternoon. We found out how someone could get into the shop!

"A little doggy door!

"It's built into the shop's front door.

"It looks just like a regular door panel.

109

"A very skinny person might get through it.

"A skinny boy like Freddy, for instance."

Sammy said, "So THAT'S where he just went!

"He's inside there now, paying back some money.

"I tried to stop him, but he went too fast.

"And I'm all mixed up. I don't believe he stole anything.

"He said to wait here ... that he's coming right out ... that he'd explain."

They stood and waited. And waited some more.

About five minutes went by.

At last, part of the front door moved. The bottom panel swung out toward them.

Bit by bit, Freddy inched himself outside.

110

Sammy said, "I was getting worried, Freddy. Tell me what this is all about."

Freddy whispered, "Shhh. Let's get into your van, but don't slam the door.

"I have to tell you something ELSE first.

"Two guys are going to rob the Messy Mutts tonight!

"I think they're BOTH gone now, but I'm not sure."

Sammy whispered, "Is this a joke, Freddy? How do you know?"

Freddy whispered, "It's no joke. I heard them planning.

"Almost like they were inside the store with me."

Mrs. Tandy whispered, "Someone could have been talking in the alley ... next to the bird feeder with the microphone."

Freddy whispered, "I was just putting some money on the desk.

"I was going to come out right away.

111

"But then I heard voices, so I switched off my flashlight.

"One of the voices said, 'I'll get the truck here at seven-thirty sharp. I know how to get the door open.

"'You just be ready to clear out those shelves.'"

Freddy went on, "I waited in the dark until I heard a big truck drive away."

Dave grabbed his phone. He dialed Chief Hemster.

Quickly, the chief called the Green Forest Police. Then he drove to the Messy Mutts.

Soon, two police cars were on the way.

The police officers hid in the alley, ready to make an arrest.

At seven-thirty, the thieves' truck drove up.

It stopped at the back door. Two men got out. They sneaked into the shop.

Chapter 13:
Freddy's Story, at Last

The Green Forest police were ready for them.

They caught the thieves carrying out pet supplies.

In a few minutes, the thieves were in handcuffs and off to jail.

Sammy said, "OK, Freddy. Now tell us about the I.O.U."

Just then, ANOTHER car drove up.

Liz and Jane got out.

Sammy said, "Look, Freddy. Mrs. Peters is here.

"Now you can tell her what happened, face to face."

Freddy began. "Well, Monday night I ... "

But ANOTHER car drove up. Dr. Jerome got out.

He said, "Liz telephoned me to come, so here I am."

Then the Green Forest police officers came back to talk to the Woodlanders.

Then Mr. Silver came by with Sandy and her mom.

He got out of his car and said, "Hello,

Freddy! What luck finding you here!

"You did such a good job today ... Could you work for us next Sunday?

"Say, what's this big crowd doing here?"

Sammy looked around.

There were seven cars ...

and seventeen people

... and Monkey in Freddy's arms.

Sammy thought, "This block looks like a carnival!"

He turned to Bill and said quietly, "Freddy asked me to keep his story from his parents.

"But their apartment is right next door.

"And they're due home soon.

"Maybe we should go somewhere else to talk."

Bill said, "Why don't we all drive over to our house?"

But it was too late to keep things a

115

secret ... because ANOTHER car drove up.

Freddy groaned, "Oh, no! It's Mom and Dad!"

His folks got out of their car and walked over.

Freddy's dad said, "What's going on here?"

His mom hugged him and said, "Are you all right, son?"

Dave said, "Freddy's mixed up in some sort of mystery.

"And he just kept a store from being robbed.

"He's going to tell us about it at our house ... if it's all right with you."

The whole crowd piled into their cars.

They drove like a night-time parade to the Woodlanders' house.

Mop was so glad to see Monkey, he chased him all over the house.

The crowd paid no attention to them.

116

Everyone turned toward Freddy, to hear his story at last.

Freddy began, "Monday evening, I was out walking Monkey.

"I was waiting for my folks to get home for dinner."

"The belt I was using for a leash was pretty short.

"Suddenly, Monkey pulled away from me. He ran right through the Messy Mutts' doggie door.

"I knew I should get him out of there fast.

"I turned sideways and squeezed in after him."

Kathy said, "But Freddy! It must have been so DARK in there!"

Freddy said, "I'm lucky.

"My folks make me carry a little flashlight.

"I turned it on.

"Monkey was busy chewing off the corner of a bag.

"Pieces of dog food were falling out of it.

"I grabbed the bag away from him.

"I pushed it outside through the doggie door.

"Then I tore out a page of my assignment book.

"I wrote an I.O.U. for you, Mrs. Peters.

"My list of dog names was on the back

of it.

"I cleaned up as much dog food as I could in a hurry. I stuffed it into my pocket."

Freddy's dad said, "So that's what fell out of your pockets last time we washed clothes!"

Bill said, "It's easy to see why you called him Monkey."

Freddy went on. "Well, I pushed Monkey out the door, and squeezed myself through.

"That's the whole story ... except I had to earn money fast to pay Mrs. Peters back.

"I hope you aren't mad at me, Mrs. Peters."

Mrs. Peters said, "Mad?

"Why, Freddy! I think you're a fine boy!"

Sammy said, "Wait, you don't know

what else he did.

"See, he went into your shop again tonight.

"He left the money to pay for the dog food."

One of the Green Forest police officers said, "This boy's a real winner, Mrs. Peters.

"He saved your shop from being robbed clean!

"He heard some people planning to empty it out."

Mrs. Tandy said, "They must have been talking in the alley ... near the mike that's in the bird feeder."

Sammy said, "I bet he was scared to death. I'd have been."

Dave said, "But he waited in the dark to hear it all."

The Green Forest police officer said, "Imagine a kid that young doing what he did!"

Mrs. Peters said, "Why, Freddy, you're a hero!

"And I need a hero, someone to help me in my shop.

"Would you like to work after school a few days a week?

Freddy said, "Would I! I could buy Monkey a real leash. And toys. And a good collar. And plenty of dog food."

Then Freddy's mother said, "But Freddy, why didn't you tell us all about it?"

Freddy said, "At first I was scared. What if you thought he'd be too much trouble?

"And then when you decided I COULD keep him ... I didn't want you to change your mind."

No one noticed that Mrs. Tandy and Bill had left the room ... until Bill called from the kitchen, "PARTY TIME!"

He and Mrs. Tandy came marching into the dining room.

Mrs. Tandy had a HUGE platter of oatmeal cookies.

Bill carried two HUGE pitchers of milk ... and a pile of paper cups and napkins.

And so the Woodlanders and their company started in on the Great Cookie Feast.

And Monkey and Mop got so many cookies, their bellies almost touched the ground ... like two little Vietnamese pot-bellied pigs.